Yanosh's Island

by Yossi Abolafia

 Greenwillow Books, New York

For Susan, Ava, and Libby

Watercolor paintings were combined with a
separate black-ink line for the full-color art.
The typeface is Zapf International Medium.

Printed in Hong Kong by South China Printing Co.

First Edition   10 9 8 7 6 5 4 3 2 1

Library of Congress Cataloging-in-Publication Data

Abolafia, Yossi.   Yanosh's island.
   Summary: When Vicky and David supply
Yanosh with the nut he needs to complete
the airplane he is building, Yanosh flies
off looking for an uncharted island.
   [1. Airplanes—Fiction.
2. Islands—Fiction]   I. Title.
PZ7.A165Yan 1987   [E]   86-19462
ISBN 0-688-06816-2
ISBN 0-688-06817-0 (lib. bdg.)

Vicky and David lived in a small town near a beach. One afternoon they found a broken mechanical turtle. They took it apart to fix it, but it was so full of springs, nuts, and bolts, they couldn't make head or tail of it.

"This is a job for Yanosh," said Vicky. "He can fix anything."

Yanosh's house was right on the beach. There was a garage,
a pigeon coop, and a backyard full of old machinery scraps.

"I hope he's in his store," said Vicky. "Sometimes he locks
himself in his garage for ages and he won't come out."
"I wonder why?" asked David.
"I don't know," said Vicky.

Yanosh was in his store. He was showing some customers his latest invention—a toaster that buttered the toast. When the last customer left, Vicky spread the parts of the broken turtle out on the counter.

"I'm sorry," said Yanosh, "but the store is closed for the day."

"Please," said Vicky. "It will only take you a minute."

Yanosh didn't answer—he was staring at the toy. Suddenly he picked up one of the parts and examined it closely. "This is exactly what I have been looking for!" he exclaimed.

"Why?" asked David. "What's so special about it?"
"It's an old nut," said Yanosh, "and they don't make them like this anymore. May I have it?"
"Sure, but why do you need it?" asked Vicky.
"Come with me and I'll show you," he replied.

They followed Yanosh to his apartment behind the store. He opened a drawer and pulled out a long white scarf. "Many years ago," Yanosh began, "when I was about your age, I was playing on this very beach.

"Suddenly a flying machine appeared out of the blue and landed right at my feet. A pilot wearing a magnificent uniform jumped out. He asked me for a wrench. I ran home and got him one. He poked around in the engine, and then he leaped back into the cockpit.

"'Hop in and I'll take you for a ride,' he said.
I got in behind him and soon we were flying
over the sea. Through the mist I could see a
small island. It was incredibly beautiful and
green, with a stream running through it.
'No one knows this island,' the pilot said.
'It's not on the map. If ever you find it again
it will be yours.' He turned the plane around
and flew me back to this beach.

"He gave me his scarf and took off.
I never saw him again."

Yanosh wound the scarf around his neck.
"I have never stopped thinking about that
island," he said, "even when I grew up.
I grew a mustache and vowed never
to shave it off until I found the island again.
I taught myself how to fly a plane, and
I built one. Only one thing is missing to complete
the engine—a nut of this very type.
Now, if you'll excuse me, I have work to do."

Vicky and David sat down outside the house.
In a little while Yanosh came out, dressed in an
aviator's uniform. He hung up a sign that said
       CLOSED FOR VACATION
and locked the door.
The children followed him into the garage.

"Here it is," Yanosh said. "Now it is finished."

"Will it really fly?" asked Vicky.

"Of course," said Yanosh proudly.

David and Vicky helped him tow the plane out of
the garage, and Yanosh climbed into the cockpit.
"I want to thank you both," he said. "If you will
bring me one of my pigeons, when I find my island
I will send you a message."

The engine coughed, roared, rattled, and rumbled,
and the plane lurched up and down.
Then it rose in the air. David and Vicky watched
it disappear over the horizon before they went home.

The next morning they hurried to
the pigeon coop, but there was
no pigeon with a message.

Suddenly they heard the fluttering of wings behind them.
They turned quickly, and there was the pigeon
with a message tied to its leg.

When the pigeon landed, they carefully removed the paper. Folded inside were a few gray hairs, but no written message.

"He must have forgotten to take his pen," said Vicky. "What do you suppose this means?"

"The hairs must be from his mustache," David said.
"He said he wouldn't shave it off until he found the
island. He wants us to know that he has found it."

"That's wonderful," said Vicky. "But what will become of him?
Do you think we will ever see him again?"
They walked along for a while, thinking about Yanosh, when
suddenly they noticed smoke rising over the hill and
a delicious smell.

They climbed to the top of the hill.
Down below they spotted bits of machinery scattered
near a stream where they sometimes picnicked.

They ran down as quickly as they could.
Yanosh's uniform was hanging from a
tree by the stream.

Near it was a campfire, and fishing in the stream
stood Yanosh! He was wearing a grass skirt and
whistling cheerfully.
"Yanosh!" they exclaimed. Yanosh took down his
uniform and vanished behind some bushes.

"How did you get here?" he called.

"We walked," said David. "Your house is just over the hill."

Yanosh sat down and held his head in his hand.

"Then this is not my island," he said.

"I flew all night long, and when I saw
this beautiful place I thought I recognized
the stream, and I landed at once—right
in the middle of it.

"First thing, I wanted to shave off my mustache but I had forgotten my razor. I knew you'd understand that the hairs in the note meant I'd found my island. But now I see that I've made a mistake. I haven't found my island at all."

"But you built a plane that really flew," said Vicky. "You should be proud of yourself."

"And this place is just as good as any island," added David.

"You are right," said Yanosh. "Let's forget about
the island and have a picnic."
Yanosh fried some more fish while Vicky
picked blueberries and David gathered apples.
It was a wonderful picnic.

Then they headed for home.

Suddenly Yanosh bent down and picked up a metal hinge.

"This is just what I need for the submarine's hatch!" he cried.
"What submarine?" asked Vicky and David at the same time.
"Why, the one I am about to build," Yanosh replied. "It should be finished by next summer, and we can all look for my island together."

THE END